# The Crystal Crypt

# *The Crystal Crypt*

Philip K. Dick

Ægypan Press

This story from the January 1954 issue of *Planet Stories.*

Special thanks to Greg Weeks, Stephen Blundell, and the Online Distributed Proofreading Team (which can be found at http://www.pgdp.net).

*The Crystal Crypt*
A publication of
ÆGYPAN PRESS

www.aegypan.com

*Stark terror ruled the Inner-Flight ship on that last Mars-Terra run. For the black-clad Leiters were on the prowl . . . and the grim red planet was not far behind.*

"Attention, Inner-Flight ship! Attention! You are ordered to land at the Control Station on Deimos for inspection. Attention! You are to land at once!"

The metallic rasp of the speaker echoed through the corridors of the great ship. The passengers glanced at each other uneasily, murmuring and peering out the port windows at the small speck below, the dot of rock that was the Martian checkpoint, Deimos.

"What's up?" an anxious passenger asked one of the pilots, hurrying through the ship to check the escape lock.

"We have to land. Keep seated." The pilot went on.

"Land? But why?" They all looked at each other. Hovering above the bulging Inner-Flight ship were three slender Martian pursuit craft, poised and alert for any emergency. As the Inner-Flight ship prepared to land the pursuit ships dropped lower, carefully maintaining themselves a short distance away.

"There's something going on," a woman passenger said nervously. "Lord, I thought we were finally through with those Martians. Now what?"

"I don't blame them for giving us one last going over," a heavy-set business man said to his companion. "After all, we're the last ship leaving Mars for Terra. We're damn lucky they let us go at all."

"You think there really will be war?" A young man said to the girl sitting in the seat next to him. "Those Martians won't dare fight, not with our weapons and ability to produce. We could take care of Mars in a month. It's all talk."

The girl glanced at him. "Don't be so sure. Mars is desperate. They'll fight tooth and nail. I've been on Mars three years." She shuddered. "Thank goodness I'm getting away. If –"

"Prepare to land!" the pilot's voice came. The ship began to settle slowly, dropping down toward the tiny emergency field on the seldom visited moon. Down, down the ship dropped. There was a grinding sound, a sickening jolt. Then silence.

"We've landed," the heavy-set business man said. "They better not do anything to us! Terra will rip them apart if they violate one Space Article."

"Please keep your seats," the pilot's voice came. "No one is to leave the ship, according to the Martian authorities. We are to remain here."

A restless stir filled the ship. Some of the passengers began to read uneasily, others stared out at the deserted field, nervous and on edge, watching the three Martian pursuit ships land and disgorge groups of armed men.

The Martian soldiers were crossing the field quickly, moving toward them, running double time.

This Inner-Flight spaceship was the last passenger vessel to leave Mars for Terra. All other ships had long since left, returning to safety before the outbreak of hostilities. The passengers were the very last to go, the final group of Terrans to leave the grim red planet, business men, expatriates, tourists, any and all Terrans who had not already gone home.

"What do you suppose they want?" the young man said to the girl. "It's hard to figure Martians out, isn't it? First they give the ship clearance, let us take off, and now they radio us to set down again. By the way, my name's Thacher, Bob Thacher. Since we're going to be here awhile –"

The port lock opened. Talking ceased abruptly, as everyone turned. A black-clad Martian official, a Province Leiter, stood framed against the bleak sunlight, staring around the ship. Behind him a handful of Martian soldiers stood waiting, their guns ready.

"This will not take long," the Leiter said, stepping into the ship, the soldiers following him. "You will be allowed to continue your trip shortly."

An audible sigh of relief went through the passengers.

"Look at him," the girl whispered to Thacher. "How I hate those black uniforms!"

"He's just a Provincial Leiter," Thacher said. "Don't worry."

The Leiter stood for a moment, his hands on his hips, looking around at them without expression. "I have ordered your ship grounded so that an inspection can be made of all persons aboard," he said. "You Terrans are the last to leave our planet. Most of you are ordinary and harmless – I am not interested in you. I am interested in finding three saboteurs, three Terrans, two men and a woman, who have committed an incredible act of destruction and violence. They are said to have fled to this ship."

Murmurs of surprise and indignation broke out on all sides. The Leiter motioned the soldiers to follow him up the aisle.

"Two hours ago a Martian city was destroyed. Nothing remains, only a depression in the sand where the city was. The city and all its people have completely vanished. An entire city destroyed in a second! Mars will never rest until the saboteurs are captured. And we know they are aboard this ship."

"It's impossible," the heavy-set business man said. "There aren't any saboteurs here."

"We'll begin with you," the Leiter said to him, stepping up beside the man's seat. One of the soldiers passed the Leiter a square metal box. "This will soon tell us if you're speaking the truth. Stand up. Get on your feet."

The man rose slowly, flushing. "See here –"

"Are you involved in the destruction of the city? Answer!"

The man swallowed angrily. "I know nothing about any destruction of any city. And furthermore –"

"He is telling the truth," the metal box said tonelessly.

"Next person." The Leiter moved down the aisle.

A thin, bald-headed man stood up nervously. "No, sir," he said. "I don't know a thing about it."

"He is telling the truth," the box affirmed.

"Next person! Stand up!"

One person after another stood, answered, and sat down again in relief. At last there were only a few people left who had not been questioned. The Leiter paused, studying them intently.

"Only five left. The three must be among you. We have narrowed it down." His hand moved to his belt. Something flashed, a rod of pale fire. He raised the rod, pointing it steadily at the five people. "All right, the first one of you. What do you know about this destruction? Are you involved with the destruction of our city?"

"No, not at all," the man murmured.

"Yes, he's telling the truth," the box intoned.

"Next!"

"Nothing – I know nothing. I had nothing to do with it."

"True," the box said.

The ship was silent. Three people remained, a middle-aged man and his wife and their son, a boy of about twelve. They stood in the corner, staring white-faced at the Leiter, at the rod in his dark fingers.

"It must be you," the Leiter grated, moving toward them. The Martian soldiers raised their guns. "It *must* be you. You there, the boy. What do you know about the destruction of our city? Answer!"

The boy shook his head. "Nothing," he whispered.

The box was silent for a moment. "He is telling the truth," it said reluctantly.

"Next!"

"Nothing," the woman muttered. "Nothing."

"The truth."

"Next!"

"I had nothing to do with blowing up your city," the man said. "You're wasting your time."

"It is the truth," the box said.

For a long time the Leiter stood, toying with his rod. At last he pushed it back in his belt and signalled the soldiers toward the exit lock.

"You may proceed on your trip," he said. He walked after the soldiers. At the hatch he stopped, looking back at the passengers, his face grim. "You may go – But Mars will not allow her enemies to escape. The three saboteurs will be caught, I promise you." He rubbed his dark jaw thoughtfully. "It is strange. I was certain they were on this ship."

Again he looked coldly around at the Terrans.

"Perhaps I was wrong. All right, proceed! But remember: the three will be caught, even if it takes endless years. Mars will catch them and punish them! I swear it!"

For a long time no one spoke. The ship lumbered through space again, its jets firing evenly, calmly, moving the passengers toward their own planet, toward home. Behind them Deimos and the red ball that was Mars dropped farther and farther away each moment, disappearing and fading into the distance.

A sigh of relief passed through the passengers. "What a lot of hot air that was," one grumbled.

"Barbarians!" a woman said.

A few of them stood up, moving out into the aisle, toward the lounge and the cocktail bar. Beside Thacher the girl got to her feet, pulling her jacket around her shoulders.

"Pardon me," she said, stepping past him.

"Going to the bar?" Thacher said. "Mind if I come along?"

"I suppose not."

They followed the others into the lounge, walking together up the aisle. "You know," Thacher said, "I don't even know your name, yet."

"My name is Mara Gordon."

"Mara? That's a nice name. What part of Terra are you from? North America? New York?"

"I've been in New York," Mara said. "New York is very lovely." She was slender and pretty, with a cloud of dark hair tumbling down her neck, against her leather jacket.

They entered the lounge and stood undecided.

"Let's sit at a table," Mara said, looking around at the people at the bar, mostly men. "Perhaps that table over there."

"But someone's there already," Thacher said. The heavy-set business man had sat down at the table and deposited his sample case on the floor. "Do we want to sit with *him?*"

"Oh, it's all right," Mara said, crossing to the table. "May we sit here?" she said to the man.

The man looked up, half-rising. "It's a pleasure," he murmured. He studied Thacher intently. "However, a friend of mine will be joining me in a moment."

"I'm sure there's room enough for us all," Mara said. She seated herself and Thacher helped her with her chair. He sat down, too, glancing up suddenly at Mara and the business man. They were looking at each other almost as if something had passed between them. The man was middle-aged, with a florid face and tired, grey eyes. His hands were mottled with the veins showing thickly. At the moment he was tapping nervously.

"My name's Thacher," Thacher said to him, holding out his hand. "Bob Thacher. Since we're going to be together for a while we might as well get to know each other."

The man studied him. Slowly his hand came out. "Why not? My name's Erickson. Ralf Erickson."

"Erickson?" Thacher smiled. "You look like a commercial man, to me." He nodded toward the sample case on the floor. "Am I right?"

The man named Erickson started to answer, but at that moment there was a stir. A thin man of about thirty had come up to the table, his eyes bright, staring down at them warmly. "Well, we're on our way," he said to Erickson.

"Hello, Mara." He pulled out a chair and sat down quickly, folding his hands on the table before him. He noticed Thacher and drew back a little. "Pardon me," he murmured.

"Bob Thacher is my name," Thacher said. "I hope I'm not intruding here." He glanced around at the three of them, Mara, alert, watching him intently, heavy-set Erickson, his face blank, and this person. "Say, do you three know each other?" he asked suddenly.

There was silence.

The robot attendant slid over soundlessly, poised to take their orders. Erickson roused himself. "Let's see," he murmured. "What will we have? Mara?"

"Whiskey and water."

"You, Jan?"

The bright slim man smiled. "The same."

"Thacher?"

"Gin and tonic."

"Whiskey and water for me, also," Erickson said. The robot attendant went off. It returned at once with the drinks, setting on the table. Each took his own. "Well," Erickson said, holding his glass up. "To our mutual success."

All drank, Thacher and the three of them, heavy-set Erickson, Mara, her eyes nervous and alert, Jan, who had just come. Again a look passed between Mara and Erickson, a look so swift that he would not have caught it had he not been looking directly at her.

"What line do you represent, Mr. Erickson?" Thacher asked.

Erickson glanced at him, then down at the sample case on the floor. He grunted. "Well, as you can see, I'm a salesman."

Thacher smiled. "I knew it! You get so you can always spot a salesman right off by his sample case. A salesman always has to carry something to show. What are you in, sir?"

Erickson paused. He licked his thick lips, his eyes blank and lidded, like a toad's. At last he rubbed his mouth with his hand and reached down, lifting up the sample case. He set it on the table in front of him.

"Well?" he said. "Perhaps we might even show Mr. Thacher."

They all stared down at the sample case. It seemed to be an ordinary leather case, with a metal handle and a snap lock. "I'm getting curious," Thacher said. "What's in there? You're all so tense. Diamonds? Stolen jewels?"

Jan laughed harshly, mirthlessly. "Erick, put it down. We're not far enough away, yet."

"Nonsense," Erick rumbled. "We're away, Jan."

"Please," Mara whispered. "Wait, Erick."

"Wait? Why? What for? You're so accustomed to –"

"Erick," Mara said. She nodded toward Thacher. "We don't know him, Erick. Please!"

"He's a Terran, isn't he?" Erickson said. "All Terrans are together in these times." He fumbled suddenly at the catch lock on the case. "Yes, Mr. Thacher. I'm a salesman. We're all salesmen, the three of us."

"Then you do know each other."

"Yes." Erickson nodded. His two companions sat rigidly, staring down. "Yes, we do. Here, I'll show you our line."

He opened the case. From it he took a letter-knife, a pencil sharpener, a glass globe paperweight, a box of thumb tacks, a stapler, some clips, a plastic ashtray, and some things Thacher could not identify. He placed the objects in a row in front of him on the tabletop. Then he closed the sample case.

"I gather you're in office supplies," Thacher said. He touched the letter-knife with his finger. "Nice quality steel. Looks like Swedish steel, to me."

Erickson nodded, looking into Thacher's face. "Not really an impressive business, is it? Office supplies. Ashtrays, paper clips." He smiled.

"Oh –" Thacher shrugged. "Why not? They're a necessity in modern business. The only thing I wonder –"

"What's that?"

"Well, I wonder how you'd ever find enough customers on Mars to make it worth your while." He paused, examining the glass paperweight. He lifted it up, holding it to the light, staring at the scene within until Erickson took it out of his hand and put it back in the sample case. "And another thing. If you three know each other, why did you sit apart when you got on?"

They looked at him quickly.

"And why didn't you speak to each other until we left Deimos?" He leaned toward Erickson, smiling at him. "Two men and a woman. Three of you. Sitting apart in the ship. Not speaking, not until the check-station was past. I find myself thinking over what the Martian said. Three saboteurs. A woman and two men."

Erickson put the things back in the sample case. He was smiling, but his face had gone chalk white. Mara stared down, playing with a drop of water on the edge of her glass. Jan clenched his hands together nervously, blinking rapidly.

"You three are the ones the Leiter was after," Thacher said softly. "You are the destroyers, the saboteurs. But their lie detector – Why didn't it trap you? How did you get by that? And now you're safe, outside the check-station." He grinned, staring around at them. "I'll be damned! And I really thought you were a salesman, Erickson. You really fooled me."

Erickson relaxed a little. "Well, Mr. Thacher, it's in a good cause. I'm sure you have no love for Mars, either. No Terran does. And I see you're leaving with the rest of us."

"True," Thacher said. "You must certainly have an interesting account to give, the three of you." He looked around the table.

"We still have an hour or so of travel. Sometimes it gets dull, this Mars-Terra run. Nothing to see, nothing to do but sit and drink in the lounge." He raised his eyes slowly. "Any chance you'd like to spin a story to keep us awake?"

Jan and Mara looked at Erickson. "Go on," Jan said. "He knows who we are. Tell him the rest of the story."

"You might as well," Mara said.

Jan let out a sigh suddenly, a sigh of relief. "Let's put the cards on the table, get this weight off us. I'm tired of sneaking around, slipping –"

"Sure," Erickson said expansively. "Why not?" He settled back in his chair, unbuttoning his vest. "Certainly, Mr. Thacher. I'll be glad to spin you a story. And I'm sure it will be interesting enough to keep you awake."

They ran through the groves of dead trees, leaping across the sun-baked Martian soil, running silently together. They went up a little rise, across a narrow ridge. Suddenly Erick stopped, throwing himself down flat on the ground. The others did the same, pressing themselves against the soil, gasping for breath.

"Be silent," Erick muttered. He raised himself a little. "No noise. There'll be Leiters nearby, from now on. We don't dare take any chances."

Between the three people lying in the grove of dead trees and the City was a barren, level waste of desert, over a mile of blasted sand. No trees or bushes marred the smooth, parched surface. Only an occasional wind, a dry wind eddying and twisting, blew the sand up into little rills. A faint odor came to them, a bitter smell of heat and sand, carried by the wind.

Erick pointed. "Look. The City – There it is."

They stared, still breathing deeply from their race through the trees. The City was close, closer than they had ever seen it before. Never had they gotten so close to it in times past. Terrans were never allowed near the great Martian cities, the centers of Martian life. Even in ordinary times, when there was no threat of approaching war, the Martians shrewdly kept all Terrans away from their citadels, partly from fear, partly from a deep, innate sense of hostility toward the white-skinned visitors whose commercial ventures had earned them the respect, and the dislike, of the whole system.

"How does it look to you?" Erick said.

The City was huge, much larger than they had imagined from the drawings and models they had studied so carefully back in New York, in the War Ministry Office. Huge it was, huge and stark, black towers rising up against the sky, incredibly thin columns of ancient metal, columns that had stood wind and sun for centuries. Around the City was a wall of stone, red stone, immense bricks that had been lugged there and fitted into place by slaves of the early Martian dynasties, under the whiplash of the first great Kings of Mars.

An ancient, sun-baked City, a City set in the middle of a wasted plain, beyond groves of dead trees, a City seldom seen by Terrans – but a City studied on maps and charts in every War Office on Terra. A City that contained, for all its ancient stone and archaic towers, the ruling group of all Mars, the Council of Senior Leiters, black-clad men who governed and ruled with an iron hand.

The Senior Leiters, twelve fanatic and devoted men, black priests, but priests with flashing rods of fire, lie detectors, rocket ships, intra-space cannon, many more things the Terran Senate could only conjecture about. The Senior Leiters and their subordinate Province Leiters – Erick and the two behind him suppressed a shudder.

"We've got to be careful," Erick said again. "We'll be passing among them, soon. If they guess who we are, or what we're here for –"

He snapped open the case he carried, glancing inside for a second. Then he closed it again, grasping the handle firmly. "Let's go," he said. He stood up slowly. "You two come up beside me. I want to make sure you look the way you should."

Mara and Jan stepped quickly ahead. Erick studied them critically as the three of them walked slowly down the slope, onto the plain, toward the towering black spires of the City.

"Jan," Erick said. "Take hold of her hand! Remember, you're going to marry her; she's your bride. And Martian peasants think a lot of their brides."

Jan was dressed in the short trousers and coat of the Martian farmer, a knotted rope tied around his waist, a hat on his head to keep off the sun. His skin was dark, colored by dye until it was almost bronze.

"You look fine," Erick said to him. He glanced at Mara. Her black hair was tied in a knot, looped through a hollowed-out yuke bone. Her face was dark, too, dark and lined with colored ceremonial pigment, green and orange stripes across her cheeks. Earrings were strung through her ears. On her feet were tiny slippers of perruh hide, laced around her ankles, and she wore long translucent Martian trousers with a bright sash tied around her waist. Between her small breasts a chain of stone beads rested, good-luck charms for the coming marriage.

"All right," Erick said. He, himself, wore the flowing grey robe of a Martian priest, dirty robes that were supposed to remain on him all his life, to be buried around him when he died. "I think we'll get past the guards. There should be heavy morning traffic on the road."

They walked on, the hard sand crunching under their feet. Against the horizon they could see specks moving, other persons going toward the City, farmers and peasants and merchants, bringing their crops and goods to market.

"See the cart!" Mara exclaimed.

They were nearing a narrow road, two ruts worn into the sand. A Martian hufa was pulling the cart, its great sides wet with perspiration, its tongue hanging out. The cart was piled high with bales of cloth, rough country cloth, hand dipped. A bent farmer urged the hufa on.

"And there." She pointed, smiling.

A group of merchants riding small animals were moving along behind the cart, Martians in long robes, their faces hidden by sand masks. On each animal was a pack, carefully tied on with rope. And beyond the merchants, plodding dully along, were peasants and farmers in an endless procession, some riding carts or animals, but mostly on foot.

Mara and Jan and Erick joined the line of people, melting in behind the merchants. No one noticed them; no one looked up or gave any sign. The march continued as before. Neither Jan nor Mara said anything to each other. They walked a little behind Erick, who paced with a certain dignity, a certain bearing becoming his position.

Once he slowed down, pointing up at the sky. "Look," he murmured, in the Martian hill dialect. "See that?"

Two black dots circled lazily. Martian patrol craft, the military on the outlook for any sign of unusual activity. War was almost ready to break out with Terra. Any day, almost any moment.

"We'll be just in time," Erick said. "Tomorrow will be too late. The last ship will have left Mars."

"I hope nothing stops us," Mara said. "I want to get back home when we're through."

Half an hour passed. They neared the City, the wall growing as they walked, rising higher and higher until it seemed to blot out the sky itself. A vast wall, a wall of eternal stone that had felt the wind and sun for centuries. A group of Martian soldiers were standing at the entrance, the single passage-gate hewn into the rock, leading to the City. As each person went through the soldiers examined him, poking his garments, looking into his load.

Erick tensed. The line had slowed almost to a halt. "It'll be our turn, soon," he murmured. "Be prepared."

"Let's hope no Leiters come around," Jan said. "The soldiers aren't so bad."

Mara was staring up at the wall and the towers beyond. Under their feet the ground trembled, vibrating and shaking. She could see tongues of flame rising from the towers, from the deep underground factories and forges of the City. The air was thick and dense with particles of soot. Mara rubbed her mouth, coughing.

"Here they come," Erick said softly.

The merchants had been examined and allowed to pass through the dark gate, the entrance through the wall into the City. They and their silent animals had already disappeared inside. The leader of the group of soldiers was beckoning impatiently to Erick, waving him on.

"Come along!" he said. "Hurry up there, old man."

Erick advanced slowly, his arms wrapped around his body, looking down at the ground.

"Who are you and what's your business here?" the soldier demanded, his hands on his hips, his gun hanging idly at his waist. Most of the soldiers were lounging lazily, leaning against the wall, some even squatting in the shade. Flies crawled on the face of one who had fallen asleep, his gun on the ground beside him.

"My business?" Erick murmured. "I am a village priest."

"Why do you want to enter the City?"

"I must bring these two people before the magistrate to marry them." He indicated Mara and Jan, standing a little behind him. "That is the Law the Leiters have made."

The soldier laughed. He circled around Erick. "What do you have in that bag you carry?"

"Laundry. We stay the night."

"What village are you from?"

"Kranos."

"Kranos?" The soldier looked to a companion. "Ever heard of Kranos?"

"A backward pig sty. I saw it once on a hunting trip."

The leader of the soldiers nodded to Jan and Mara. The two of them advanced, their hands clasped, standing close together. One of the soldiers put his hand on Mara's bare shoulder, turning her around.

"Nice little wife you're getting," he said. "Good and firm-looking." He winked, grinning lewdly.

Jan glanced at him in sullen resentment. The soldiers guffawed. "All right," the leader said to Erick. "You people can pass."

Erick took a small purse from his robes and gave the soldier a coin. Then the three of them went into the dark tunnel that was the entrance, passing through the wall of stone, into the City beyond.

They were within the City!

"Now," Erick whispered. "Hurry."

Around them the City roared and cracked, the sound of a thousand vents and machines, shaking the stones under their feet. Erick led Mara and Jan into a corner, by a row of brick warehouses. People were everywhere, hurrying back and forth, shouting above the din, merchants, peddlers, soldiers, street women. Erick bent down and opened the case he carried. From the case he quickly took three small coils of fine metal, intricate meshed wires and vanes worked together into a small cone. Jan took one and Mara took one. Erick put the remaining cone into his robe and snapped the case shut again.

"Now remember, the coils must be buried in such a way that the line runs through the center of the City. We must trisect the main section, where the largest concentration of buildings is. Remember the maps! Watch the alleys and streets carefully. Talk to no one if you can help it. Each of you has enough Martian money to buy your way out of trouble. Watch especially for cut-purses, and for heaven's sake, don't get lost."

Erick broke off. Two black-clad Leiters were coming along the inside of the wall, strolling together with their hands behind their backs. They noticed the three who stood in the corner by the warehouses and stopped.

"Go," Erick muttered. "And be back here at sundown." He smiled grimly. "Or never come back."

Each went off a different way, walking quickly without looking back. The Leiters watched them go. "The little bride was quite lovely," one Leiter said. "Those hill people have the stamp of nobility in their blood, from the old times."

"A very lucky young peasant to possess her," the other said. They went on. Erick looked after them, still smiling a little. Then he joined the surging mass of people that milled eternally through the streets of the City.

At dusk they met outside the gate. The sun was soon to set, and the air had turned thin and frigid. It cut through their clothing like knives.

Mara huddled against Jan, trembling and rubbing her bare arms.

"Well?" Erick said. "Did you both succeed?"

Around them peasants and merchants were pouring from the entrance, leaving the City to return to their farms and villages, starting the long trip back across the plain toward the hills beyond. None of them noticed the shivering girl and the young man and the old priest standing by the wall.

"Mine's in place," Jan said. "On the other side of the City, on the extreme edge. Buried by a well."

"Mine's in the industrial section," Mara whispered, her teeth chattering. "Jan, give me something to put over me! I'm freezing."

"Good," Erick said. "Then the three coils should trisect dead center, if the models were correct." He looked up at the darkening sky. Already, stars were beginning to show. Two dots, the evening patrol, moved slowly toward the horizon. "Let's hurry. It won't be long."

They joined the line of Martians moving along the road, away from the City. Behind them the City was losing itself in the somber tones of night, its black spires disappearing into darkness.

They walked silently with the country people until the flat ridge of dead trees became visible on the horizon. Then they left the road and turned off, walking toward the trees.

"Almost time!" Erick said. He increased his pace, looking back at Jan and Mara impatiently.

"Come on!"

They hurried, making their way through the twilight, stumbling over rocks and dead branches, up the side of the ridge. At the top Erick halted, standing with his hands on his hips, looking back.

"See," he murmured. "The City. The last time we'll ever see it this way."

"Can I sit down?" Mara said. "My feet hurt me."

Jan pulled at Erick's sleeve. "Hurry, Erick! Not much time left." He laughed nervously. "If everything goes right we'll be able to look at it – forever."

"But not like this," Erick murmured. He squatted down, snapping his case open. He took some tubes and wiring out and assembled them together on the ground, at the peak of the ridge. A small pyramid of wire and plastic grew, shaped by his expert hands.

At last he grunted, standing up. "All right."

"Is it pointed directly at the City?" Mara asked anxiously, looking down at the pyramid.

Erick nodded. "Yes, it's placed according –" He stopped, suddenly stiffening. "Get back! It's time! *Hurry!*"

Jan ran, down the far side of the slope, away from the City, pulling Mara with him. Erick came quickly after, still looking back at the distant spires, almost lost in the night sky.

"Down."

Jan sprawled out, Mara beside him, her trembling body pressed against his. Erick settled down into the sand and dead branches, still trying to see. "I want to see it," he murmured. "A miracle. I want to see –"

A flash, a blinding burst of violet light, lit up the sky. Erick clapped his hands over his eyes. The flash whitened, growing larger, expanding. Suddenly there was a roar, and a furious hot wind rushed past him, throwing him on his face in the sand. The hot dry wind licked and seared at them, crackling the bits of branches into flame. Mara and Jan shut their eyes, pressed tightly together.

"God –" Erick muttered.

The storm passed. They opened their eyes slowly. The sky was still alive with fire, a drifting cloud of sparks that was beginning to dissipate with the night wind. Erick stood up unsteadily, helping Jan and Mara to their feet. The three of them stood, staring silently across the dark waste, the black plain, none of them speaking.

The City was gone.

At last Erick turned away. "That part's done," he said. "Now the rest! Give me a hand, Jan. There'll be a thousand patrol ships around here in a minute."

"I see one already," Mara said, pointing up. A spot winked in the sky, a rapidly moving spot. "They're coming, Erick." There was a throb of chill fear in her voice.

"I know." Erick and Jan squatted on the ground around the pyramid of tubes and plastic, pulling the pyramid apart. The pyramid was fused, fused together like molten glass. Erick tore the pieces away with trembling fingers. From the remains of the pyramid he pulled something forth, something he held up high, trying to make it out in the darkness. Jan and Mara came close to see, both staring up intently, almost without breathing.

"There it is," Erick said. "There!"

In his hand was a globe, a small transparent globe of glass. Within the glass something moved, something minute and fragile, spires almost too small to be seen, microscopic, a complex web swimming within the hollow glass globe. A web of spires. A City.

Erick put the globe into the case and snapped it shut. "Let's go," he said. They began to lope back through the trees, back the way they had come before. "We'll change in the car," he said as they ran. "I think we should keep these clothes on until we're actually inside the car. We still might encounter someone."

"I'll be glad to get my own clothing on again," Jan said. "I feel funny in these little pants."

"How do you think I feel?" Mara gasped. "I'm freezing in this, what there is of it."

"All young Martian brides dress that way," Erick said. He clutched the case tightly as they ran. "I think it looks fine."

"Thank you," Mara said, "but it is cold."

"What do you suppose they'll think?" Jan asked. "They'll assume the City was destroyed, won't they? That's certain."

"Yes," Erick said. "They'll be sure it was blown up. We can count on that. And it will be damn important to us that they think so!"

"The car should be around here, someplace," Mara said, slowing down.

"No. Farther on," Erick said. "Past that little hill over there. In the ravine, by the trees. It's so hard to see where we are."

"Shall I light something?" Jan said.

"No. There may be patrols around who –"

He halted abruptly. Jan and Mara stopped beside him. "What –" Mara began.

A light glimmered. Something stirred in the darkness. There was a sound.

"Quick!" Erick rasped. He dropped, throwing the case far away from him, into the bushes. He straightened up tensely.

A figure loomed up, moving through the darkness, and behind it came more figures, men, soldiers in uniform. The light flashed up brightly, blinding them. Erick closed his eyes. The light left him, touching Mara and Jan, standing silently together, clasping hands. Then it flicked down to the ground and around in a circle.

A Leiter stepped forward, a tall figure in black, with his soldiers close behind him, their guns ready. "You three," the Leiter said. "Who are you? Don't move. Stand where you are."

He came up to Erick, peering at him intently, his hard Martian face without expression. He went all around Erick, examining his robes, his sleeves.

"Please –" Erick began in a quavering voice, but the Leiter cut him off.

"I'll do the talking. Who are you three? What are you doing here? Speak up."

"We – we are going back to our village," Erick muttered, staring down, his hands folded. "We were in the City, and now we are going home."

One of the soldiers spoke into a mouthpiece. He clicked it off and put it away.

"Come with me," the Leiter said. "We're taking you in. Hurry along."

"In? Back to the City?"

One of the soldiers laughed. "The City is gone," he said. "All that's left of it you can put in the palm of your hand."

"But what happened?" Mara said.

"No one knows. Come on, hurry it up!"

There was a sound. A soldier came quickly out of the darkness. "A Senior Leiter," he said. "Coming this way." He disappeared again.

"A Senior Leiter." The soldiers stood waiting, standing at a respectful attention. A moment later the Senior Leiter stepped into the light, a black-clad old man, his ancient face thin and hard, like a bird's, eyes bright and alert. He looked from Erick to Jan.

"Who are these people?" he demanded.

"Villagers going back home."

"No, they're not. They don't stand like villagers. Villagers slump – diet, poor food. These people are not villagers. I myself came from the hills, and I know."

He stepped close to Erick, looking keenly into his face. "Who are you? Look at his chin – he never shaved with a sharpened stone! Something is wrong here."

In his hand a rod of pale fire flashed. "The City is gone, and with it at least half the Leiter Council. It is very strange, a flash, then heat, and a wind. But it was not fission. I am puzzled. All at once the City has vanished. Nothing is left but a depression in the sand."

"We'll take them in," the other Leiter said. "Soldiers, surround them. Make certain that –"

"Run!" Erick cried. He struck out, knocking the rod from the Senior Leiter's hand. They were all running, soldiers shouting, flashing their lights, stumbling against each other in the darkness. Erick dropped to his knees, groping frantically in the bushes. His fingers closed over the handle of the case and he leaped up. In Terran he shouted to Mara and Jan.

"Hurry! To the car! Run!" He set off, down the slope, stumbling through the darkness. He could hear soldiers behind him, soldiers running and falling. A body collided against him and he struck out. Someplace behind him there was a hiss, and a section of the slope went up in flames. The Leiter's rod –

"Erick," Mara cried from the darkness. He ran toward her. Suddenly he slipped, falling on a stone. Confusion and firing. The sound of excited voices.

"Erick, is that you?" Jan caught hold of him, helping him up. "The car. It's over here. Where's Mara?"

"I'm here," Mara's voice came. "Over here, by the car."

A light flashed. A tree went up in a puff of fire, and Erick felt the singe of the heat against his face. He and Jan made their way toward the girl. Mara's hand caught his in the darkness.

"Now the car," Erick said. "If they haven't got to it." He slid down the slope into the ravine, fumbling in the darkness, reaching and holding onto the handle of the case. Reaching, reaching –

He touched something cold and smooth. Metal, a metal door handle. Relief flooded through him. "I've found it! Jan, get inside. Mara, come on." He pushed Jan past him, into the car. Mara slipped in after Jan, her small agile body crowding in beside him.

"Stop!" a voice shouted from above. "There's no use hiding in that ravine. We'll get you! Come up and –"

The sound of voices was drowned out by the roar of the car's motor. A moment later they shot into the darkness, the car rising into the air. Treetops broke and cracked under them as Erick turned the car from side to side, avoiding the groping shafts of pale light from below, the last furious thrusts from the two Leiters and their soldiers.

Then they were away, above the trees, high in the air, gaining speed each moment, leaving the knot of Martians far behind.

"Toward Marsport," Jan said to Erick. "Right?"

Erick nodded. "Yes. We'll land outside the field, in the hills. We can change back to our regular clothing there, our commercial clothing. Damn it – we'll be lucky if we can get there in time for the ship."

"The last ship," Mara whispered, her chest rising and falling. "What if we don't get there in time?"

Erick looked down at the leather case in his lap. "We'll have to get there," he murmured. "We must!"

For a long time there was silence. Thacher stared at Erickson. The older man was leaning back in his chair, sipping a little of his drink. Mara and Jan were silent.

"So you didn't destroy the City," Thacher said. "You didn't destroy it at all. You shrank it down and put it in a glass globe, in a paperweight. And now you're salesmen again, with a sample case of office supplies!"

Erickson smiled. He opened the briefcase and reaching into it he brought out the glass globe paperweight. He held it up, looking into it. "Yes, we stole the City from the Martians. That's how we got by the lie detector. It was true that we knew nothing about a *destroyed* City."

"But why?" Thacher said. "Why steal a City? Why not merely bomb it?"

"Ransom," Mara said fervently, gazing into the globe, her dark eyes bright. "Their biggest City, half of their Council – in Erick's hand!"

"Mars will have to do what Terra asks," Erickson said. "Now Terra will be able to make her commercial demands felt. Maybe there won't even be a war. Perhaps Terra will get her way without fighting." Still smiling, he put the globe back into the briefcase and locked it.

"Quite a story," Thacher said. "What an amazing process, reduction of size – A whole City reduced to microscopic dimensions. Amazing. No wonder you were able to escape. With such daring as that, no one could hope to stop you."

He looked down at the briefcase on the floor. Underneath them the jets murmured and vibrated evenly, as the ship moved through space toward distant Terra.

"We still have quite a way to go," Jan said. "You've heard our story, Thacher. Why not tell us yours? What sort of line are you in? What's your business?"

"Yes," Mara said. "What do you do?"

"What do I do?" Thacher said. "Well, if you like, I'll show you." He reached into his coat and brought out something. Something that flashed and glinted, something slender. A rod of pale fire.

The three stared at it. Sickened shock settled over them slowly.

Thacher held the rod loosely, calmly, pointing it at Erickson. "We knew you three were on this ship," he said. "There was no doubt of that. But we did not know what had become of the City. My theory was that the City had not been destroyed at all, that something else had happened to it. Council instruments measured a sudden loss of mass in that area, a decrease equal to the mass of the City. Somehow the City had been spirited away, not destroyed. But I could not convince the other Council Leiters of it. I had to follow you alone."

Thacher turned a little, nodding to the men sitting at the bar. The men rose at once, coming toward the table.

"A very interesting process you have. Mars will benefit a great deal from it. Perhaps it will even turn the tide in our favor. When we return to Marsport I wish to begin work on it at once. And now, if you will please pass me the briefcase –"

www.ingramcontent.com/pod-product-compliance
Lightning Source LLC
LaVergne TN
LVHW090619110826
845146LV00001B/451

* 9 7 8 1 4 6 3 8 0 1 9 3 9 *